CW01263038

MY CHRISTMAS GIFT ARE YOU

Novel by

SELVAGGIA STARK

Copyright © 2024 SELVAGGIA STARK

All Rights Reserved This work is published directly by the author and the author retains all exclusive rights. No part of this book may be reproduced without prior permission of the author.

I DEDICATE THIS NOVEL TO MY HUSBAND GIANDOMENICO.
HE WAS AND ALWAYS WILL BE MY CHRISTMAS PRESENT.
-SELVAGGIA STARK-

CHAPTER 1

The car sped down the tree-lined avenue leading into the English town.

Felicity watched from the window. She loved this time of year; the air was crisp and full of love.

The avenue led to the main street, which was now lit by thousands of Christmas lights.

All along the way, the trees were decorated with glittering garlands of lights and colorful baubles, with a predominance of white, red, and green, creating a magical and joyful atmosphere.

From the windows of the houses you could see handmade Christmas decorations, such as bright stars, colorful candles, angels in flight and little Santas, which gave the houses a touch of personality and originality.

Felicity felt like she was in a real Christmas village, with people happily walking by with packages. It was her favorite time of the year. She enjoyed feeling the first chill on her skin, cooking soups with seasonal vegetables, and putting on her first sweaters to keep warm from the air that was beginning to feel cooler.

Unfortunately, she was there because her beloved grandmother had died and she could not miss her funeral.

Looking at the streets and shops, he had to admit that his small town had changed somewhat. Some new facades of international brands had replaced small local shops The car with the driver was now on the main road, and she could see that her favorite store, "Norma's Cafeteria," with its red sign, was there. As she walked past it, she was reminded of when she used to go there every Sunday as a child to enjoy her chocolate and cream, and then, as she got older, she used to go there with her friends on those cold afternoons when people wanted to get together.

Dear Norma, the owner of the café, was always waiting for them with her unfailing, loving smile. Norma knew them all by name and had seen them born and raised. These girls, now teenagers, came to her.

Norma was a woman who had lived through many painful situations in her life, such as World War II; sometimes, Sometimes she said this even though she was very small. She still remembered the sound of the sirens and how she ran into the cellar to hide from the German bombing. She was a woman with a great personality, with an intelligent and sharp look, her hair was now silver, which she kept in a big bun, she loved to wear many stone necklaces of a thousand colors.. around her neck and wore wide, colorful dresses.

She always wore her ubiquitous red-rimmed glasses, which were attached to a colorful chain around her neck.

She always said that without that chain she would have lost her glasses a thousand times over. She was fond of the cafeteria it was This cafeteria, which they all thought was magical, was a place where customers who stopped in and enjoyed its specialties, suddenly felt serene, at peace with themselves and safe. Even Felicity and her friends, when they went there together, drinking their cup of hot chocolate, cup of hot chocolate, felt happiness and joy and in that harmonious environment they confided their first loves. she owned that establishment for many years.

At the thought of that memory, Felicity shivered with nostalgia. How she missed these moments.

The car turned down a side street and stopped in front of a white house. She had arrived!

The English-style house exuded a warm and inviting atmosphere. The exterior walls were painted a pure white color, which gave the building a refined and elegant appearance. In addition, the guillotine windows and wooden windowsills added a touch of elegance to the house.

Now, at Christmas time, the cottage was adorned with an array of decorations that made it even more enchanting. A handmade Christmas wreath with pine branches and red bows was placed on the front porch, and delicate lights placed on the porch railings created a magical atmosphere.

The windows were adorned with festoons of flashing lights, giving the outside a warm and festive glow. On the cottage's sloping roof, a cute miniature Santa Claus was positioned as if he were coming down the chimney to bring gifts.

The front yard was decorated with figurines, including reindeer pulling a sleigh full of presents and snowmen.

As she got out of the car, Felicity was enchanted by the sight. Once again, she had not been able to help Tom and her father with the decorations.

The driver took the case and looked at her; she smiled and walked to the front door.

It was cold this late afternoon. Felicity shrugged her shoulders to warm up a bit and wrapped the scarf around her neck.

After a few minutes, the door opened and her mother's face appeared. She hugged her. Behind her was her father, who caressed her and then happily left the house to pick up her suitcase from the driver who had remained in the driveway.

It was cold that late afternoon. Felicity shrugged her shoulders to warm up a bit and wrapped the scarf around her neck.

After a few minutes, the door opened, and the mother's face showed up. She hugged her. Behind her was her father, who gave her a caress and then happily left the house to retrieve her suitcase from the driver who had remained on the driveway.

It was cold on that late afternoon. Felicity tightened her shoulders to warm up a bit and wrapped her scarf tightly around her neck.

Felicity entered the house with her mother, took off her coat, and positioned herself in front of the lit fireplace to warm up a little, meanwhile looking around. In that room, too, all the Christmas decorations had already been put up, such as the large garland on the fireplace with large gold bows, the Christmas fir tree decorated with a thousand gold-colored bulbs, and a myriad of balls of many colors that the family had bought at various Christmas markets in past years.

Looking at all this in his heart, he felt an immense nostalgia. And she thought of their London apartment, completely devoid of any sign of Christmas.

Father closed the door and took his suitcase to her room, which was upstairs, then hurried downstairs, not wanting to miss a moment, his little girl was back and in his heart there was boundless joy.

"I'm going to make you some tea. Is that okay, Felicity?" Her mother's voice rang out in the silence, where only the crackling of wood in the fire could be heard. She turned and replied, "Yes, Mom, thank you."

Meanwhile, her father returned from upstairs and sat down in his chair by the fireplace and looked at his daughter and asked, "How was the trip?" Felicity, now warmed by the fire, sat down and lay down on the couch, she liked to do that, it reminded her of when she was a child, before going to bed in her pajamas, she would lie in that position and listen to her grandmother read her a fairy tale.

"Well, luckily the train was on time and everything was quiet!!!"

"I'm glad you could come," Mom said, coming out of the kitchen with a tray of Christmas cups and cookies. Felicity looked at the fire in the fireplace. She replied with a sad expression, "Grandma, I heard from her a few days ago; she seemed fine. Mom replied with a sad tone, "She had a weak heart, Felicity.

Now they were all sitting on the couch. Suddenly the doorbell rang. Everyone looked at each other with a curious expression. Who was it? They were not expecting anyone.

CHAPTER 2

Felicity's mother went to open the door, after which an exclamation was heard from the front room. "Hello, how nice to see you, come in, Felicity has just arrived, put your coat down, would you like a cup of tea?" after these words the person her mother was talking to finally appeared and Felicity could not believe her eyes, it was Mary, her best friend, when she saw her she went over to her and they hugged happily.

. Felicity, catching her breath with excitement, asked as she sat down, "But how did you know I had arrived?" Mary also took a seat on the large sofa in front of the blazing fireplace and took the small mug that was handed to her and replied with a smile and a mischievous look, "I saw you driving by, I had just come out of our cafeteria and saw your beautiful face through the car window and so I decided to join you here at your home and it has been a long time since we have heard and seen each other," Felicity shook his free hand contentedly and replied, " I'm sorry and that I've had a very exhausting time in the art gallery that we have on the calendar these months, several exhibitions with very well known artists and I've been so busy, cataloguing the paintings and exhibiting them with all that it entails is really hard work".

The group, in front of the fireplace and a thousand lit Christmas lights, in this sweet and loving atmosphere, talked about many things, including the place where Grandma's funeral would take place and the preparations and especially the refreshments that would be served. would be held afterwards in honour of the late grandmother.

The two friends after drinking their tea set out for Felicity's room and upon entering had a heart attack, her mom had not changed anything in her room since she left everything had remained as Felicity had left it the day she left.

The two girls looked at each other in disbelief and smiled smugly.

Mary sat down on the bed while Felicity opened her suitcase to arrange her things. The girl looked at her and asked, "Looking at your suitcase, I get the feeling you won't be staying long, will you?" She took a few sweaters and looked at them, noticing her friend's "sad expression and reluctantly replied, " No, Mary, I can't be away from work too long, you know, my boss, who knew about Grandma, didn't object to my sudden departure, but he made me understand not to stay any longer than I had to. "Then she resumed opening drawers and putting her things away.

Mary looked sadly out of the window and said with an enraptured and absorbed look, "Felicity, I think it's going to snow soon. On the way here I felt the itch in my nose that I always get before it starts to snow. my personal thermometer "and touched her nose, both of them laughed.

Felicity finished arranging her clothes and lay down on the bed next to her friend and they held hands and their heads touched, like when they were little, they would spend whole afternoons on the bed together reading or confiding secrets to each other or dreaming about what they would do when they grew up.

Felicity was a girl with thick golden hair, she had beautiful long straight blonde hair, tall and slim, she loved to dress sporty and casual with jeans or pants paired with colorful sweaters. She loved cashmere, she loved to wear such soft sweaters. At work she had to wear a full skirt and jacket or pants with a jacket and unfortunately shoes with high heels which she did not like very much, in fact she found them uncomfortable.

When she had to go home on the subway, she carried very comfortable sneakers in her bag to change her shoes, and there her feet finally said thank you!

She had beautiful green sharp-looking eyes, a regular face, and a beautiful full mouth that was the envy of all her friends. She didn't need to put on lipstick; she had strong pink lips. She loved art.

Mary was a little shorter, with brown hair and glasses, she liked to dress casually and loved to play sports, she was very good at ice skating.

Friends since primary school, they had been inseparable until Felicity suddenly decided to leave for that job at the art gallery in London, it had not been easy for Mary to part with Felicity, but she understood that her friend wanted to get out of that small quiet town and try new things.

Unlike her, who was happy there, she had no desire to live in a big city, her dream was to become a teacher and practice in her hometown school one day.

Side by side they stood in silence, how many things they would have liked to say to each other, but now both of them just had to stand close and look out of the large window of the room, now the sky had turned gray, and looking at the movement of the plants, they noticed that a nice wind had come up.

"Maybe you are right Mary, I think we are going to get a good snowfall in a while."

Suddenly barking was heard from downstairs and the door to the room suddenly opened to reveal the family dog, Buddy, a golden retriever breed, who leapt onto the bed with a bound and threw himself at Felicity, filling her with licks, screams and laughter filled the room, shortly after which Felicity's brother Tom walked in.

Wearing his field hockey team jacket, she tried to get Buddy off the bed, but he would not budge from his mistress, then after a while, tired Buddy calmed down and lay down under Felicity's bed, happy and content.

Everyone caught their breath. Felicity went to hug her brother, who was in the middle of the room looking at her with a big, happy smile. They hugged for a while; it had been a long time since they had seen each other. Then suddenly Tom's face changed. Breaking away from his sister, he said as he walked to his room across the hall. "Finally you came; it took Grandma's death for you to come," he said in an angry tone.

Tom would not have wanted his sister to go to London. Despite being two years younger, he had always been very protective of Felicity.

When she heard those words she was hurt and she said, "Stop saying those things, you know I work a lot and I'm the gallery director," but Tom didn't answer and he went to his room. The two girls looked at each other and Mary grimaced, "You know how much he misses you, right? He felt responsible for you from childhood, remember when we all played together, he was always in the front row defending you from anyone who bullied you? Sometimes he would take a beating for you" Felicity heard these words and walked to the window not wanting to be seen by her friend but Mary knew she understood what she was feeling so she got out of bed and walked over to her and leaned on her shoulder to comfort her.

CHAPTER 3

Tom entered his room and threw his coat on the bed and sat down at his desk, he was still angry with his sister, seeing her again made him feel that anger for leaving him alone.

Sure, they talked on the phone and made a few video calls, but being close was another thing.

He still did not understand her decision, why she had left so quickly.

He had not believed the story about wanting to work in an art gallery, he knew that her dream was not to be an ordinary art gallery manager, his parents on the other hand had no doubted about his choice, he on the contrary knew there was something else behind it.

After her has sister left for London he had asked around if anything special had happened to Felicity to make her to leave so quickly, but nothing had come up , silence.

Tom looked in the mirror, he was tired, he had just finished his practice with his small town field hockey team of which he was captain.

He had loved ice skating from a young age, thanks to his grandfather, who had been British champion field hockey player in his youth and had passed on his passion to his grandson. He had trained him from an early age and saw great potential in him, and so slowly, practice after practice, he had become the captain of his team, which was now climbing the ranks. Tom had a powerful build and tall stature, light brown hair and deep brown eyes, a face with the typical features of a person with a strong and determined personality, who liked to dress up casually and wore sportswear, but of famous brands As he looked at the screen of the PC thinking about all these things, he heard a knock at the door and called out, "Who is it?" "It's me," Felicity replied as she slowly walked in, he turned and looked at her and motioned for her to sit in the chair, Felicity, a little intimidated, sat down and smiled at Tom, "So how's life going big brother?" he stood up and took off his team jersey and replied without looking at her, "Good, the team is doing great and in a little while if we win two more games we will move up to the pro ranks," Felicity let out a yell, "Good job, Grandpa knew you would be a champion and a pro in this sport..." silence.

Tom pretended not to have heard those words; he was still angry. He opened the closet and took out a light blue sweater and put it on. Felicity asked him, "I've never seen that sweater before. Who gave it to you?" He blushed a little. When he went to the bathroom, he replied, "Karen." She frowned and replied, "Karen, and who is that?"

"If you were more present in my life, you would know that, don't you think?" And he went into the bathroom and closed the door"

Felicity did not answer, she got up and decided to go back to her room. Mary was waiting for her and when she saw her coming she asked, "So you talked to Tom?" The girl replied with a somewhat disappointed face, "I decided to talk to him after the funeral and better, now he is too tired and angry." Mary looked at her watch and said, "I have to go. My mother is waiting for me," and waving goodbye, she gave him a kiss on the cheek, but first she asked, "I'll see you tomorrow morning for breakfast, I'll pick you up, let's go to the cafeteria, okay?" Felicity replied happily, "Yeah, all right. See you tomorrow." Mary closed the door happily and heard her footsteps coming down the stairs and the door closing.

Alone in the room, she sat down at her desk, picked up her laptop, and turned it on. The mailbox was full. Oh, Mamma Mia, I have to work!!! After a while she heard her mother calling her, tiredly she closed her laptop and looked out of the big window, noticing that it was dark now, she went downstairs.

Alone in the room, she sat down at her desk, picked up her laptop, and turned it on. The mailbox was full. Oh, Mamma Mia, I have to work!!!

After a while she heard her mother calling her, tiredly she closed her laptop and looked out of the big window, noticing that it was dark now, she went downstairs.

"Dinner is ready!" Felicity looked at the clock above the fireplace and realized that she had been working for a good two hours! The dining room table was set, her father was watching TV while Tom was listening to music on his cell phone, as she entered the kitchen she smelled the smells of her mother's cooking, she grabbed a piece of bread, and she began to eat bread and dipped it into the soup that was still simmering on the stove, her mother looked at her and smiled, it was her vice to taste the food before eating it ever since she was a child she would enter the kitchen and run and take the bread and taste everything on the stove.

"Delicious, Mom. You made the pumpkin and potato soup that I like." Mom approached, kissed her little nose as she used to when she was little, and replied, "Of course, I made it for you." All four of them now sat down to eat. Tom barely looked at his sister, and she tried to avoid his gaze. She did not want to find herself arguing at the table; it was something she could not stand. "So, Felicity, tell us about London. I'm sorry, but your boss, what's his name?" her father asked as he took a sip of wine, Felicity replied boredly, it was the umpteenth time he told her, "Sam's name is Dad and she's a woman. ""Yes Sam, is she still hateful or has she calmed down?" She looked at him in amazement, her father was like that, he got straight to the point.

Jhon, that was her father's name, had been the best car salesman in the area for several years, he knew people at first glance when he saw them., he could even see a refrigerator at the North Pole. He had met her mother one day when she entered the car dealership where she worked looking for a car; Jhon, seeing her enter, struck by her beauty, said to his colleague, "Let me take care of this," and so he married her a year later. As they say, love at first sight, for her mother it was the same, when she entered, she saw a handsome, well-dressed young man with beautiful blue eyes, which struck her, coming towards her, and from that moment she knew that for him she would buy any car, the important thing was that he was in it. This is what her mother used to tell him. And yes! Looking at them after a good thirty years, you could tell they were still in love, Felicity admired them and was a little jealous of the lasting and strong love her parents had. "So, Felicity, did you hear?" her father asked, she came back to reality and replied, "Well, Dad, what can I tell you? You'd say she's a pain in the ass, I'll tell you she's a bit of a handful," and everyone laughed, including her father who waved his glass to make a toast, "To grandma, rest in peace and allow us to come together," and they all shouted, "To grandma..." She went to bed early, tired. She put on her pretty pink super plush pajamas and climbed into her bed. How wonderful it was to be in her room! She felt like a little girl again. How sweet to feel cuddled and loved, the love that only a family can give.

Someone knocked on her door and a moment later Tom came in in his pajamas, she saw him come in and was startled and immediately said, "Tom please, I don't want to fight. Tom nodded and said, "No

Felicity, I don't want to fight with you. I just want you to be more honest with me," she looked at him questioningly and said, "What do you mean?" he sat down on the bed and said, "I want you to tell me the real reason why you left," he was speechless, how had he realized that the real reason was something else? However, she did not feel like telling him the truth at that moment, so she looked at him affectionately and simply said, "Good night big brother, sleep well," he resignedly got out of bed and went back to his room.

Felicity would have liked to confide in Tom but did not feel like going over that bitter chapter of her life. With so much difficulty, she had metabolized it and tried to hide it in the depths of her heart, where it had to stay. Her eyes full of memories turned to the garden, suddenly she saw small snowflakes falling from the sky, she jumped up and went to the window. How wonderful the snow, she opened her hand out and small flakes landed on it and wet her hand, she felt a thrill of excitement, she loved winter.

With the window still open she took a long breath she adored that fresh air ,she looked at her garden small snowflakes were covering the grass and plants with a light white mantle ,the lights of the lit Christmas decorations made the atmosphere even more magical, how she would have liked to spend Christmas with her parents but Willy's exhibition was opening right at Christmas ,a sense of sadness filled her heart and like a little girl taking away a present, she closed the window and went back to bed , turned off the light and fell asleep while outside the snow continued to fall slowly covering everything even the past?

Chapter 4

" Felicity " her mother's voice woke her up she opened her eyes and with a snap she went to the window and saw that the landscape was now completely covered in snow, like a happy child she quickly went downstairs and was surprised to find herself in front of Mary who was waiting for her in the living room, the two women looked at her with a surprised look, Mary said "But you're still in your pajamas??don't you remember that we have to have breakfast together?" Felicity looked at the clock in the hall and saw that it was ten o'clock. she waved for them to wait and, turning around, ran up the stairs to change.

The two women left watching Felicity's performance looked at each other and laughed, "She's such a good sleeper," they exclaimed. "Here I am!" After a few minutes, she reappeared, dressed in jeans, boots, and a white cashmere sweater. She greeted her mother and they went to the cafeteria.

Now the city was completely blanketed in snow, but the roads had been cleared during the night and it was safe to walk. The air was filled with the sweet scent of cinnamon, thanks to the shops that spread the typical aroma of freshly baked panettone and warm Christmas drinks. The shop windows were decorated with twinkling lights, miniature Christmas trees and tiny reindeer that seemed to be dancing on the snow.

Walking down the avenue felt like being immersed in a real Christmas village. People passed by happily laden with gift packages, the car occupants stopping occasionally to admire the decorations and take souvenir photographs.

Felicity liked the atmosphere that the snow left on things and in the air. The two girls walked slowly. Mary began to tell him about the

University that was ending. She listened, but as she walked, she observed herself around her, and the scenery of celebration and joy filled her heart with energy and happiness.

On the way, she met some people who knew her. Some offered condolences for her grandmother, and many asked how she was doing in London. Eventually, they arrived at the Cafeteria.

Arriving in front of the cafeteria entrance, she stopped excitedly to look at that red door with the sign saying "Cafeteria da Norma." In the window, there were already Christmas decorations. She smiled happily and opened the door. Upon entering the cafeteria, she was immediately enveloped by the inviting aromas of freshly ground coffee, freshly baked pastries, cinnamon, cocoa, and ginger. The décor featured dark wood tables, giving the atmosphere a rustic and warm feel. The walls were decorated with pine garlands, twinkling lights, and Christmas-themed decorations. The predominant colors were red and green, creating a festive and joyful atmosphere.

Each table had a Christmas centerpiece such as small Christmas trees and scented candles that filled the room with a mixture of scents.

The dim lights and candles created an intimate and relaxing atmosphere, perfect for enjoying a quiet moment. The cafeteria counter was also decorated with a large Christmas wreath, complete with gold bells that tinkled softly when the door was opened.

The cafeteria menu offered a wide variety of hot beverages such as tea, coffee, and hot chocolate, as well as cakes, cookies, and holiday treats. Many of the cakes and drinks featured flavors and ingredients characteristic of the holiday season, such as cinnamon, ginger, and citrus. She walked in, and it seemed to her that she was entering a magical and unreal place, entranced she was speechless, suddenly she heard a voice behind her "Felicity, how glad I am to see you...I've been waiting for you" Turning around she saw the lovely Norma standing next to her with her sweet smile, they embraced. Norma took her hand and together they walked to her favorite coffee table.. The woman sat down with the two girls. Felicity, happy to be back in this place, asked Norma, "Do you always make my favorite croissant?" Norma closed her eyes to concentrate and after a few seconds said, "I bet it's the one with blackberry jam, isn't it?" Felicity said in surprise, "That's right, Norma, you are a miracle! With all the people who come here, you remembered my favorite croissant?" she smiled and motioned for the waitress to bring two cappuccinos and two croissants. Then Nora became a bit more serious and said, taking Felicity's hand, "I am so sorry about your grandmother, I had seen her a few days ago, she had come to visit me, honestly I had seen her a bit tired. And then two days ago, I heard that she had gone to heaven," after saying these words with a sad face, she got up and went to the counter.

The front door had a small bell that rang when someone came in or went out, it was always the same all these years, it had a loud but sweet sound at the same time.

Suddenly, the bell rang. At that moment, Felicity was conversing with Mary. Her face was not turned to the doorway, but that sound seemed different than usual, so instinctively, she turned to the door, and her heart stopped in surprise.

It was him, it was him she could not believe her eyes. Andrew was the last person she wanted to see.

The boy in the blue jacket walked in without noticing the two girls' presence. With customary manners, he sat down at the counter, ordered a coffee, and took a croissant from the tray. Felicity stood motionless with the cup in her hand. Mary looked at her and understood and said to him in a low voice, "I wanted to tell you that Andrew is back and here for a few days. I think he has started working at his father's real estate office. "Felicity lowered the cup and her eyes did not want to see him. "Andrew, have you seen who's back? Felicity," Norma's voice echoed in the bar; he turned to see the two girls, his gaze remained motionless, without expression, he did not know what to do. Norma, unaware of what she had just done, said to him from the bar"Come on, go say hello to her, you were such friends," she said, pushing him towards the table with her hand. He got up and walked slowly towards the two girls; Felicity looked up and stared into his eyes, but said nothing. She was stuck. Andrew looked around to see if they were watching him, and said ,"Hi Felicity, how are you? ""Hi Felicity, how are you?" she gazed at him and replied "Good, very good actually, and you?" he said, putting his hands in his pockets. and shrugs his shoulders in his characteristic way. Well, I've been back for a while. I started working with my father."

Silence, no one spoke, Mary, realizing that the situation could escalate on Felicity's part, made a decision and said, "Maybe it's better to go , Felicity," had not stopped looking at him. He looked around, intimidated. Mary grabbed their jackets, took her by the arm, and pushed her toward the door. They went out. Andrew watched them leave with a guilty and sorry expression. Norma came out of the kitchen and noticed that the two girls were no longer sitting at their table she ran up the street looking for them, when she saw them down the street she called out "Felicity I need to talk to you can you come over to my house tonight?" She turned and nodded, and when the woman returned, wondering why they had left without saying goodbye, he walked over to their table to clean up and saw that they had not even finished drinking their cappuccino. Then, suspicious, she looked up and saw Andrew at the counter drinking his coffee; she picked things up from the table and walked over to him with the tray and asked, "Look Andrew, did you say something wrong? Because they left like two thieves." He replied without looking up, "I don't know, maybe they had things to do," but Norma noticed that his face had turned red after saying that. She returned to the kitchen with many questions in her head but no answers. Andrew's heart was pounding, he had managed to remain calm but inside he was agitated, he had not expected to see her, her legs were shaking with excitement. He had heard that his grandmother had died, but he had not thought that she might come back; he knew that she worked a lot, so he had believed that she would not have time to come back, and instead there she was, as beautiful as ever, and with that look in her eyes that had stopped his heart. "Felicity, you have to forget him, you understand someone like him, it's better not to have anything to do , he's caused you too much pain, you have to ignore him as if he wasn't there." All these things Mary said to her as they walked home at a fast pace "Felicity felt so much anger inside that she could not listen to what her friend was saying to her, she was too nervous and in her mind she only had Andrew's face. They arrived at Felicity's house, she said goodbye to her friend and went inside, Mary stood outside the door with a desolate look on her face, she was sorry for what had happened, now she felt a little guilty for taking her to the cafeteria, but how could she have known that Andrew would arrive? Sad about what had happened, she walked home. Felicity's house was empty except for Buddy who, seeing her enter, went to meet her and celebrate, but she did not even notice him. She ran up the stairs and into his room, threw herself on the bed and began to cry. A loud and desperate cry, how could she have believed in him?

How could she love him? How could she follow him?

CHAPTER 5

After crying she fell asleep exhausted from all the emotions she had felt. She reopened her eyes, looked at the clock and realized that she had slept for a couple of hours, still sleepy she went out of her room and down the stairs, in the living room were her parents who were reading in front of the fireplace, Buddy heard her coming and came up to him, this time the girl caressed him then went into the kitchen to get something to drink, light snowflakes could be seen falling from the window, then she went into the living room. She fell asleep exhausted after all the emotions she had felt. She opened her eyes again and looked at the clock and realized that she had slept for a couple of hours, still sleepy she went out of her room and down the stairs, in the living room were her parents who were reading in front of the fireplace, Buddy heard her coming and went up to him, this time the girl caressed him then went to the kitchen to get something to drink, from the window light snowflakes could be seen falling, c

When she came into the living room, her mother said to her, "You are so tired! I went upstairs when I came in and saw you sleeping soundly, I didn't want to wake you. Come here and sit with us for a while." With these words she sat down next to her mother and put her head on her mother's shoulder, she was in great need of being cuddled. "I saw Norma and she told me to remind you to stop by her place after the service this afternoon," her father's words echoed in the silence, she looked at him and replied, "Ah yes, I forgot, of course I will stop by," then she looked at her mother with a sad look and asked him, "Mom, what shall I wear today, I don't have anything black," her mother with a look of someone who always has to solve everything opened a box and pulled out a very nice new dress of black color and I put it on her. Felicity stood up and admired him. He looked really cute with the dress in his hand, and suddenly he began to cry.

His grandmother, Carol, had always been close to him; before he was born, she had knitted him a blanket with her own hands, which she still had. She took her to school and packed her lunch when her parents were working. After school, Felicity was always with her at her house. They were very close. Sometimes Felicity thought she was closer to her grandmother than to her mother. Whenever she had a problem or doubt, she would go to her grandmother. She would listen carefully and then gently give her opinion, and in the end, her advice was always the best.

The funeral took place in the early afternoon, it had begun to snow, and as we all walked to the cemetery, Felicity thought that her grandmother would like the soft, white snow.

Norma was among those present, a true friend of Grandmother's, even though they were a few years younger and had spent their teenage years together, and then both had married twins they had met together.

After the ceremony was over, everyone went to Felicity's house for refreshments. Many people had attended, and she was much loved by all. "Felicity, I'm going home now. I'll wait for you when you're done here, okay?" Norma asked. Felicity looked at her at the front door and nodded, and Norma walked out of the house, encouraged.

The family thanked everyone, and when the last person left, they tidied up the house.

CHAPTER 6

The doorbell rang, Norma opened the door and saw Felicity still dressed in her black ceremony dress and coat, "Come in," Norma said and made her sit down in the living room, in the center of the room was a large lit fireplace, in a corner near the window was a black colored grand piano, sometimes Norma played it. Nearby was positioned an antique sideboard where leaning were some photos, Felicity intrigued approached and looked at a black and white photo in which were depicted two young women embracing smiling at the lens and she recognized her grandmother so she asked Norma who was standing next to her "Are you two real when you were young?" she smilingly took the photo with the silver frame and answered "Yes, that's us. We were always together before we got married, night and day. We completed each other. I was more impetuous and she was more calm and rational, we helped each other, we loved each other like two sisters. And tears fell from her face, which she wiped away with a white handkerchief she had in her sweater pocket". But now let's sit down, I have to give you an envelope," Felicity looked at her with a curious expression. An envelope! Nervously, Felicity sat on the sofa and watched as the woman walked over to the antique sideboard and opened a drawer, taking out an unopened white envelope and handing it to her.

Felicity's hands trembled as she took it and read, "To my beloved granddaughter, my last will and testament."

As she read the words, she began to cry.

Norma encouraged her, "Come on, read it.

Felicity opened it.

Only the sound of the clock hands could be heard in the room.

During the reading of the letter, Norma stood by her side.

After writing it Felicity looked with a surprised look at Norma.

Norma after she finished reading it felt empowered to speak

Felicity, I know you don't understand, but your grandmother wrote this will because she loved you very much.

The girl got up with the letter in her hand and went to the window. It was still snowing. The snowflakes were bigger now, coming down and covering everything with their whiteness.

Some little birds were sheltering from the cold in a little house that Norma had built for them and in which she had also put seeds to feed them. How wonderful to see all this. She turned and looked at Norma and said, "Did you know about this?" The woman nodded yes, stood up and approached her,

"Few people know that the coffee shop was also your grandmother's; only the lawyer and the notary public handled the sale. Your grandmother had invested everything she had and given me the responsibility of running it. At the end of the month, we were making half the profits.

Now, she has left it to you. I'm getting old for that job, and I'd be happy for you to take over the Cafeteria."

Those words seemed like a boulder to her. Her work in London? The art gallery? She couldn't leave it all behind; she had responsibilities. She looked at the woman with a confused look as she looked at her with her sweet and pleading eyes, but now Felicity did not feel like giving an answer so she said "Norma is an important decision for me, I would like to think about it a bit" Hearing these words the woman smiled and hugged her saying "I understand, but would you like to come and help me tomorrow morning in the cafeteria?

Felicity seemed like a good proposal, she would work in the Cafeteria , since she still had a few days left and then she would decide. With a satisfied smile she gave her hand to Norma and shook it saying "Okay deal, I'll be there tomorrow morning" Norma shook her hand in satisfaction and said "I'll be waiting for you at 7 o'clock, we have to prepare the croissants" Felicity's eyes widened "7 o'clock? I have a feeling it's going to be a busy day, she said as she left the house.

Felicity raised her face and snowflakes bathed her face, she felt confused but also excited, maybe something was changing in her life?

Chapter 7

Felicity walked out of Norma's house and looked up at the sky, the snow was slowly falling, closed her coat tightly, and putting on her hat, she walked home.

From a distance, he saw the lights on in the hall of his house, entered, and found his entire family gathered there.

They watched her enter, she waved goodbye and after removing her coat and leaving her snow-soaked boots at the entrance she walked into the room, the fireplace warmth warming her from the cold.

Everyone looked at her, intrigued by this meeting with Norma, and waited for Felicity to say something.

"Did you know that Grandma had a 50% stake in the cafeteria at Norma's?"

Everyone said in unison, "NOOO."

"Well, now you know, this is the will she left for Norma to give to me," she said, handing the letter to her mother. Everyone moved next to her so they could read it together. Felicity, meanwhile, looked at the fire in the fireplace and thought it was bitter cabbage now. Did her grandmother want her to work there and move back to live near her family and London? Silence, then her mother's voice, "It's a surprise to everyone, my mother never told me anything, it's amazing all these years she's kept it a secret," she looked at her daughter and said, "Now it's your turn! She loved you so much and knew you, she always knew what was best for you from a young age, sometimes she was more perceptive than I was as your mother," everyone's eyes turned to Felicity who was motionless as if hypnotized by the fire.perceptive than me being your mother" everyone's gaze turned "I know, Mom, but I have a duty to Sam and the gallery; I gave my word."

His father, who had been silent, said, "Honey, wait to decide, think about it, you still have a few days to decide. Felicity replied, "Yes indeed, Dad, tomorrow morning I have decided to go to the cafeteria, Norma is expecting me at seven o'clock and we are going to start making croissants together and I must say the idea tickles me," Tom laughed and said, "Leave some for the customers, Sister? Don't eat them all" knowing everyone knew she was very greedy they looked at her and Felicity with a look of discouragement said "Too bad I'll have to leave some if not what is poor Norma selling?" and they all laughed as the letter stood there in her mania waiting for an answer

In her bed before falling asleep, she imagined herself in the cafeteria taking orders and preparing breakfast and strangely enough, she did not mind the idea who knows?

Then she fell asleep with a smile on her face, thinking of all the croissants she would make and even eat the next morning.

CHAPTER 8

Felicity woke up early that morning, got up and went to the bathroom to wash up, then returned to her room to get dressed, the whole family was still asleep.

She went downstairs and went into the kitchen, looked out the window, it was still dark, you could just see the reflection of the streetlight on the white snow. She drank a nice cup of coffee and ate a cookie that his mother had made with nuts, she tasted it and closed his eyes and thought, "What goodness!!!"

Meanwhile, Buddy had joined her in the kitchen and wagged his tail and asked her with his begging snout for a cookie, she gave him the cookie and he munched and made a big noise and ate it she smiled to see him so happy, then finished breakfast, looked at the clock and it was almost 7 o'clock, so she went to the door, put on her boots, coat, hat and scarf and gloves and went out.

The air was cold with a light breeze that cooled her nose.

She wrapped the scarf around her face and walked on. When she arrived in front of the diner, she saw that the door had been left slightly open and a light could be glimpsed from the kitchen, she went in and the little bell rang, to Felicity it seemed to greet her. Norma came out in her pastry apron and greeted her, "Well Felicity, you're right on time, close the door and follow me." She walked into the kitchen and was enchanted: the kitchen was a cozy and charming place; in the center was a fireplace that gave a warm and familiar atmosphere with the fire burning. The walls were decorated with beautiful yellow tiles, and the floor was covered with wooden panels that made the room cozy. The sweet and inviting smell of Christmas cakes filled the air; a wooden table dominated the center of the kitchen, where doughs of soft white flour, fresh eggs, fragrant butter and sugar were carefully prepared and poured into jars.

Norma, seeing Felicity enchanted and enraptured by this scene, said, "Here the doughs are prepared with love and care, following old family recipes handed down from generation to generation. In the middle of the table was an old recipe book, now open.. Above the stove stood a pair of gleaming copper pots in which Norma gently heated chocolate. The woman took a wooden ladle and carefully stirred the mixture until it reached a velvety, creamy consistency. The smell of chocolate suddenly mingled with the typical Christmas aromas of cinnamon, ginger, and vanilla chocolate, creating a symphony of scents in the room. Felicity scanned the kitchen and noticed that pans and molds of all shapes and sizes were positioned in every corner of the kitchen, ready to hold the perfectly formed dough. Norma moved deftly, filling the pans with dough and decorating some of the pans with molds with candied fruit, nuts, and powdered sugar, ready to be baked in the wood stove.

With great care she opened the oven and inserted two prints of previously prepared doughnuts and asked Felicity to join her, she approached fascinated and leaned over the oven to see the flames of the fire dancing and embracing the doughnuts, Norma set the stopwatch to make sure each cake was baked just right. While the cakes were baking in the oven she told Felicity to change, in fact she was still in her coat, she went at the woman's direction to get an apron and found a pink one with her name on it, surprised she looked at Norma who was watching her as she deftly rolled out the dough for the croissants and answered her thoughts, "Your grandmother had made it a few days before she died it was her gift to you". Felicity was moved and took the apron and after clutching it to her heart she put it on and a feeling of well-being invaded her soul and mind.

The girl caught up with Norma and admired the skill and dexterity in working the puff pastry for the croissants, then she told the girl to take two wheels that were next to the cookbook and together, following her advice, they began to cut the dough into triangles and then put the filling in the center of each triangle. Carefully, they rolled each triangle from the base until they had the characteristic shape of croissants. The filling was the famous jams that Norma made.

Once this stage was completed, Norma placed the croissants on a baking sheet lined with parchment paper and brushed them with egg yolk to make them golden brown during baking. First, however, he removed the two prints for the doughnuts and then baked the baking sheets with the croissants in a preheated oven at 180 degrees for about 15 to 20 minutes, or until the croissants were puffed and golden. When the doughnuts cooled, he placed the two cakes on two trays decorated with white lace and red ribbon, ready to be displayed in the cafeteria windows. Delicious croissants were ready to welcome customers and delight the palates of anyone who stopped by.

Glancing at the clock Norma decided to open and walked out the front door, she put out the board with the day's menu and turned on all the lights, outside the sky was incredibly pink, today was going to be a beautiful day, the day was already ready to be admired and reflect its sun rays on the blanket of snow.

Felicity looked out the diner window and was excited, perhaps this day was an omen for a new future?

The little bell rang. Here is the first customer.

Chapter 9

Jessica Norma's helper arrived soon after and showed her how to set and clear a table and how to use the Italian coffee machine, which made excellent espressos. The morning passed quickly; her friend Mary also came to visit.

At lunchtime Felicity was in the kitchen with Norma making sandwiches when she heard the little bell, came out of the kitchen and was confronted by two blue eyes staring at her.

Her heart stopped for a moment and she stood motionless looking at the young man in a sports jacket who was sitting at the counter watching her with surprise.

"Excuse me, are you new?" she said holding a glass, "Yes, my name is Felicity," he asked smiling, "Hi Felicity, could you ask Norma to pack my lunch for me? "She looked at him, she had never seen such a scary good looking guy before.

Light brown hair of medium length, blue eyes and a smile that would your breath away.

Hearing the boy's voice, Norma came out of the kitchen holding her lunch pack and smiling I posed it to the mystery boy, he got up from the stool to walk to the cash register Felicity could see that he was very tall and with two good shoulders she imagined him without clothes and a shiver invaded her body.

Not realizing what he had done to Felicity, he went to the cashier and talked with Norma for a while, then paid and thanked her, but before he left he looked at Felicity, and he squeezed his eye and waved her off.

At this point Felicity feared she was going to faint, her legs had gone soft, but fortunately she clung to the counter and stood still, waiting for her body to regain strength.

Norma looked at her with a look of amusement, realizing that this boy had impressed her, so she asked him, "Do you know who he is?" She said in a whisper, "NO" The woman leaned closer and said, "He's Alex, the new coach of Tom's jockey team.

Suddenly her cell phone rang, she kept it in her bag in the kitchen, but the ringtone was so loud that they could hear it in the hall, the customers turned to her and she blushed apologetically and went to the kitchen to answer it, saw the name Sam on the screen and answered.

"Hello Felicity, can you hear me? " The ringing, nervous voice of her boss could be heard loud and clear.

"Yes Sam, I can hear you, tell me," her boss was probably calling her as she was driving, "Felicity, the whole office is looking for Willy's papers for the exhibit and we can't find them, where did you put them," Felicity was getting nervous, but she was trying to control herself. "Sam, like all the documents I keep are in my desk drawer, they are in a red folder." Sam replied, "We'll be expecting you before the exhibition, don't play games with me Felicity, you're in charge of the Gallery, you promised me you'd be gone for a few days, I'll be expecting you in a couple of days, take care," and threw down the phone.

At that moment, he had the urge to throw his cell phone in the croissant oven, but then he took a deep breath and tried to find the calm again.

"Felicity, you can go, that leaves Jessica. Rest if you want, I'll see you in the morning," Norma told him as she entered the kitchen with a satisfied face at Felicity's work. You did a really good job, congratulations.

Felicity still held the cell phone, put it in her pocket and went to hug Norma, "Thank you Norma," she took her coat and waved to the customers, she knew almost all of them, and Felicity came out with a happy and satisfied face.

As she walked, she thought about the day she had just had and her experience in the cafeteria, absorbed in her thoughts, she did not notice that her brother was next to her, "Hi big sis, I wanted to visit you but I was late for practice," she turned around and saw her brother with his gym bag and wearing his team jacket looking at her with a happy smile, in her heart she hoped that her sister could return home with this opportunity in the cafeteria.

She looked at him and was reminded of the space hottie she had seen in the cafeteria and asked him in a low voice, "Listen Tom, did your coach come over to get his lunch?" Tom looked at her and replied, "A yes!!Alex, he always comes over to get his sandwich at Norma's." "I didn't know you had a new coach?" said Felicity.

He stopped and looked at her and said, "Excuse me, but where do you live now and where have you lived all these months? You don't know many things!"

She took him under her arm and walked with him, saying, "You're right, let's try to catch up, shall we? Now tell me about this Alex," and leaning her head on her brother's shoulder like when they were little, he began to tell happily.

Chapter 10

He has been coming for a couple of months, replacing the old coach who is now elderly, so one day we find this handsome hunk coming in and he starts giving orders. We in the team looked at him with curiosity, we asked him who he was, he was surprised that no one had warned him of his arrival, he said "Well I'm your new coach, my name is Alex", all my teammates looked at each other, he seemed a little young to be a coach, but then he started giving orders and giving us warm-ups and talking about game tactics and that's when we knew he was a smart guy who knew his stuff.

Felicity listened very carefully and when he finished, Felicity looked at him with a disappointed look and asked, "Is that all? Is that all you know?" The brother looked at his sister and suddenly realized what she wanted to know and smiled at him, "AHH I get it, do you like it?" she suddenly pulled away from her brother and replied with a red face, "No, what are you thinking? It's just curiosity" but he looked her at them and continued to tease her them, so they started throwing snowballs and chasing each other all the way home.

They went through the door, still laughing, but their mother, who heard them entering the house, stopped them on the threshold and told them to take off their snow-covered shoes and put everything by the fireplace. Looking at each other and smiling, they did as their mother said and placed their boots and coats next to the fireplace, which was lit.

Exhausted, they collapsed and sat on the sofa, looking at each other happily, holding hands and smiling: they had regained their attunement.

Felicity then went up to her room to change and turned on her PC, she had a lot of work emails, she sat down but had no desire to answer them, she was tired, the work in the cafeteria was challenging but very tiring, so she lay down on the bed and without noticing she fell asleep with a smile on her lips, maybe she was dreaming of Alex?

CHAPTER 11

"Felicity is here Mary" the sound of her mother's voice suddenly woke her and she opened her eyes with difficulty she replied "Mother have her come into the room" Mary entered and found her half asleep on the bed and smiling she sat down beside her and said "It's hard working in the cafeteria isn't it?"

She got up to change, replied, "Yes but also very funny," and with a sly look went to the bathroom to put on a warm suit.

When she returned she saw Mary with a thoughtful look looking out of the window she approached her and asked "Is something wrong?" she turned to her friend and said "Andrew came this morning to the library where I go to study" at those words Felicity had a tremor and sat down in her chair while her friend remained standing and stroked her hair, she always did this when she was nervous thought Felicity""And what did he want from you?" Mary shrugged and said, "Well, at first he pretended to be there to get a book, but then when he saw that I was ignoring him, he sat down at my desk and stared at me; I was researching for an exam, I had my face between the books, but suddenly I felt his gaze on me. I looked up and saw his big eyes staring at me, I lost my patience and asked him, "What is it Andrew, what do you want from me?

Felicity sat motionless in his chair, and his heart pounded. What did he want now? He wondered, hadn't she already done enough? Had she ruined his life, and now she wanted to annoy her friend, too?

Mary continued, "He asked me if you came here often and if you had a boyfriend." At these words Felicity jumped up from her chair and grabbed an ornament and threw it in the air, luckily it fell on the mattress. Mary saw her friend's reaction and stopped in horror, not saying another word, she had never seen her so angry. Silence in the room, Felicity looked at the bed with the object she had just thrown and Mary looked at her with her mouth open.

Felicity, a quite comical sight. Then Felicity realizing what she had done turned to Mary who was still staring at her with her mouth open and said "Excuse me Mary but my nerves are gone he asks if I am engaged after all he has done to me? How dare he come to you and ask that question. If I had him here I would punch him," and made a boxing gesture.

Mary seeing her making those strange gestures and with an angry face began to laugh it was funny to see Felicity trying to punch the air.

She saw Maria laughing and realized how funny she was. Her mother heard her laugh and smiled as well, "The usual." And she went back to preparing dinner.

Calm returned. Mary continued the story "At those questions from Alex I was speechless I didn't know what to answer him so I told him that I didn't know anything and that he should ask you directly."

"Good, "said Felicity patting Mary's shoulder, "That's the way to do it, I really want to see if she has the courage to come to me and ask me."

Chapter 12

Felicity sat in her chair after Mary left, despite the anger she felt inside, she still had the memory of that day when they decided to run away together.

"Come on Felicity, why don't we run away together?" Andrew's face had turned red with eagerness and desire to run away together. Felicity looked at him as if she saw him for the first time, "What do you mean run away together? It's not like we're living in the Middle Ages where you had to elope to get engaged." And he got up from his bench in the park, it was spring and nature was awakening with all its power. She picked up her books and walked down the path, Andrew looked at her and ran after her.

"Let's get organized, now that we've finished college we can get a job in London and without saying anything we'll live together,"

Felicity stopped at those words and looked at him carefully to see if he was joking or serious "To leave here, why?" and he kissed her hard and kept his face on hers answering him "To be together, you know here they would look at us a little strangely, here couples get engaged and then get married cohabitation is looked at badly .

I think your parents would feel the same way, and so would my father. So the only way is for us to get jobs separately and then find each other in London and live together without saying a word!" After saying that he hugged her so tightly that Felicity couldn't breathe for a moment. The girl was speechless, no one knew they were together, they met secretly, only Mary knew and she could keep secrets.

"I'm not deciding anything now, I'll think about it."

Back home, this idea, which at first seemed silly, began to seem like an opportunity for growth and, above all, independence; by now she had finished college, there were only two exams left that she would soon take, she was majoring in art. London would be a good experience,

She began looking at job advertisements for recent graduates and, by chance, saw a job in an Art Gallery in central London. The salary was not bad, although rents were very expensive there. However, if she shared an apartment with Andrew, it would be perfect.

They met secretly and began planning, Andrew found a job in a London real estate agency with the help of a friend of his father's, and slowly the project became a reality.

Only the last stumbling block remained - her family

The whole family was in the living room when Felicity decided to break the news, after laying out her plans to leave for London and work in an art gallery, her mother looked at her with surprise and asked, "But are you sure? Living alone in a big city?" Felicity reluctantly had to tell a lie and said "No! I found a girl to share the apartment with" At these words her mother looked at her husband to see what he was thinking, but he smoked his pipe and said not a word, his gaze was fixed on his daughter. Tom, on the other hand, stood up abruptly from the chair and began to shout, "Mom, you're not going to let her go like this, it's dangerous, London is a city, she's used to being here in the family, it's a risky choice, I don't agree." And he left, walking out of the house, slamming the door hard. Everyone looked at him, then her parents turned to her and stood looking at her; at that moment she felt a feeling of doubt in her heart. Was she doing the right thing? After all, it was her first work experience after graduation, and she would be leaving her family and friends for the first time.

However, her love for Andrew took over and she continued with her decision to leave, even though she felt some doubt in her heart.

Her parents took a few days before giving him permission to call the art gallery where Felicity was hired. They talked to the boss, Sam, and then they wanted to get the address of the house where she was going to live, and indeed there was a girl there, but they did not know that she would leave after a month and that Andrew would be there instead. Felicity and Andrew had arranged everything as best they could: she would leave soon and after about a month he would join her.

Mary heard the decision to go to London and was speechless, she did not think she would lose her friend, she would have loved to spend the summer vacation together and instead she would go and with Andrew to boot.

She often saw him fooling around with other girls, and when Mary asked him to explain, he just said he was joking. But deep in her heart, she did not trust him; she would have liked to see her friend with a more mature and serious guy.

The day of departure came quickly, Felicity with her family and Mary stood on the platform of the station waiting for the train. Everyone was very sad, Tom did not want to go to say goodbye to her, he was still angry with her, but at his mother's insistence he was there. Father had not expressed a real opinion, he simply had faith in Felicity. He, too, had lived in London for some time as a young man, and the experience had made him mature and responsible and independent, and he hoped in his heart that his daughter would be the same. The gallery she was going to work for was one of the most prestigious in London, had a good reputation, was located in a charming Victorian building with a large exhibition space and an extensive art collection.

The train arrived and everyone said their goodbyes, Mary promised Felicity to visit her soon. Mother began to cry and Tom angrily gave her just a kiss on the cheek and said "Be careful big sister, don't go out alone at night and make sure you don't trust strangers" and with a serious face he looked at her, then father hugged her and gave her a kiss on the forehead and looking at her with affection he said "We will miss you a lot but if you feel like taking this step you have every right to do it." Felicity had tears in her eyes, she felt a hole in her stomach, with difficulty she got on the train and waved to the group from the window, the train pulled away and Felicity felt a huge emptiness in her heart, she sat in her seat and tears streaked her face, she could not hold them back. Now she was alone.invaded her face, she could not contain herself ..now she was alone.

Chapter 13

When she arrived in London, she found that the city was very different from what she had expected. There was a lot of hustle and bustle and the pace of life was much faster than what she was used to. The first few days were difficult.

The apartment she shared was a few blocks from the Galleria, two bedrooms, a small kitchenette, and a bathroom. The apartment was on the top floor, so when she arrived with her suitcase and saw the stairs, she felt faint. The real estate agent had forgotten to tell him that the apartment was on the 3rd floor and there was no elevator.

The girl shared the apartment with was a hostess, so she could be absent for several days.

The first day at work was a little difficult, remembering all the things to do and getting used to the hectic pace of working in an art gallery, a demanding job that required a lot of precision, but Felicity felt at home in her natural environment. She loved being around works of art, learning their history and discovering emerging artists, but' she always felt a longing for her family, her consolation being that she would soon be joined by Andrew...

Her parents called every night, and sometimes Tom joined in the greetings.

Andrew would hear from him sometimes during the week, late in the evening, saying that he had almost everything arranged for his arrival.

Mary would hear from her on weekends.

At the gallery she made some friends, her older colleague Matilde and a younger but very knowledgeable colleague named Andrew. Sometimes, after the gallery closed, they went to a pub for a beer. There, Felicity tried new foods, especially Indian food. Although it was very spicy, she liked it very much. She also discovered new places that stimulated her and opened her mind to new cultures.

One Saturday while Felicity was walking in a park near her apartment the phone rang, it was Mary calling her as she always did, "Hello Mary how are you?" on the other end of the phone there was a few moments of silence, Felicity frowned worriedly "Hello! Mary are you there? "Yes, I'm here," the girl said with a smile, "I was getting worried," Mary began to speak, but her voice was different, a lower tone and you could tell she was not well, "Mary, stop, I don't understand what you're saying to me. Calm down and breathe." Silence.

"Felicity, I have something to tell you. And it's not going to be Felicity immediately imagined that something had happened to her family and her heart stopped for a moment "Don't worry, your family is fine, it's Andrew" Felicity decided to sit down on a nearby bench at these words "What happened?" as she asked this question she realized that it had been several days since she had heard from him. It was only a few days before he arrived.

"Now promise me to be calm, you promise?" Felicity looked up at the sky and answered, "Yes Mary I promise."

"For a few days I had been seeing Andrew with Susan, they were walking together, one night I even saw them having dinner at the Italian restaurant, the fancy one. I wondered what he was doing with her. I wanted to tell you, but I didn't want to worry you. Today I heard from a friend of Susan's something you won't like." Felicity's hands shook with excitement and nervousness, "What is it now?" Mary caught her breath and said all at once, "Andrew ran off with Susan, they went to the Bahamas...."

"What did I hear? Andrew, the one who made me come here, left my family with the promise of living together and went to the Bahamas with Susan?" Mary replied in a hushed voice, "Yes."

These were difficult days for Felicity, she was completely devastated now that she knew that Andrew would not be joining her, she felt even more alone in this big city. For him, her life had been turned upside down, she had left her quiet life, her parents and friends, for Andrew...for a love she thought was mutual, after leaving everything for him, Felicity felt lost and betrayed. She had imagined a happy life together, but now she realized too late that Andrew was not the person she thought he was.

The disappointment was so deep that Felicity felt betrayed not only by him but also by herself for blindly trusting him. She was desperate to find a way out.

So she threw herself into work and fortunately there was always plenty of work. She would work late, take a cab, and when she got to her apartment, she would throw herself on the bed, exhausted, and sometimes she would not even eat, and she would find herself in the morning still wearing her clothes from the day before.

She spoke to her roommate and asked if she could kindly find a colleague to take her place. The stewardess looked at her in surprise and asked, "What about your boyfriend?" Felicity looked at her and coldly replied, "He decided to go to the Bahamas with someone else" The hostess looked at her with a knowing look and said, "Men. Okay, I'll find someone for you," and gave him a caress to let him know that she was close to her.

As she was true to her word, a colleague of Chinese nationality, very kind and sweet, came to take her place. Sometimes in the evening, when she came home late from work, she would leave some Chinese dishes in the kitchen for her.

In her heart, she had decided that she would no longer sacrifice her well-being for anyone.

Over time, Felicity became known for her passion and expertise. She began organizing solo exhibitions for young artists and developed a network of contacts in the art world. The gallery where she worked became a point of reference for art lovers in London, Felicity was proud to be part of this world, but in her heart she felt an emptiness, she had professional, hard-won success, she spent late Nights in the office, but she understood that it was all for the art world. it was not real, it was all fleeting, because after everything she came home and was alone.

Mary came to visit a few times and gave her news of Andrew, who had not yet returned from this trip; he was said to have found work as a waiter in a beach bar and the girl was working in a hotel. The families of both boys were not very happy with their behavior and it was said that they wanted to pick them up and take them back to England.

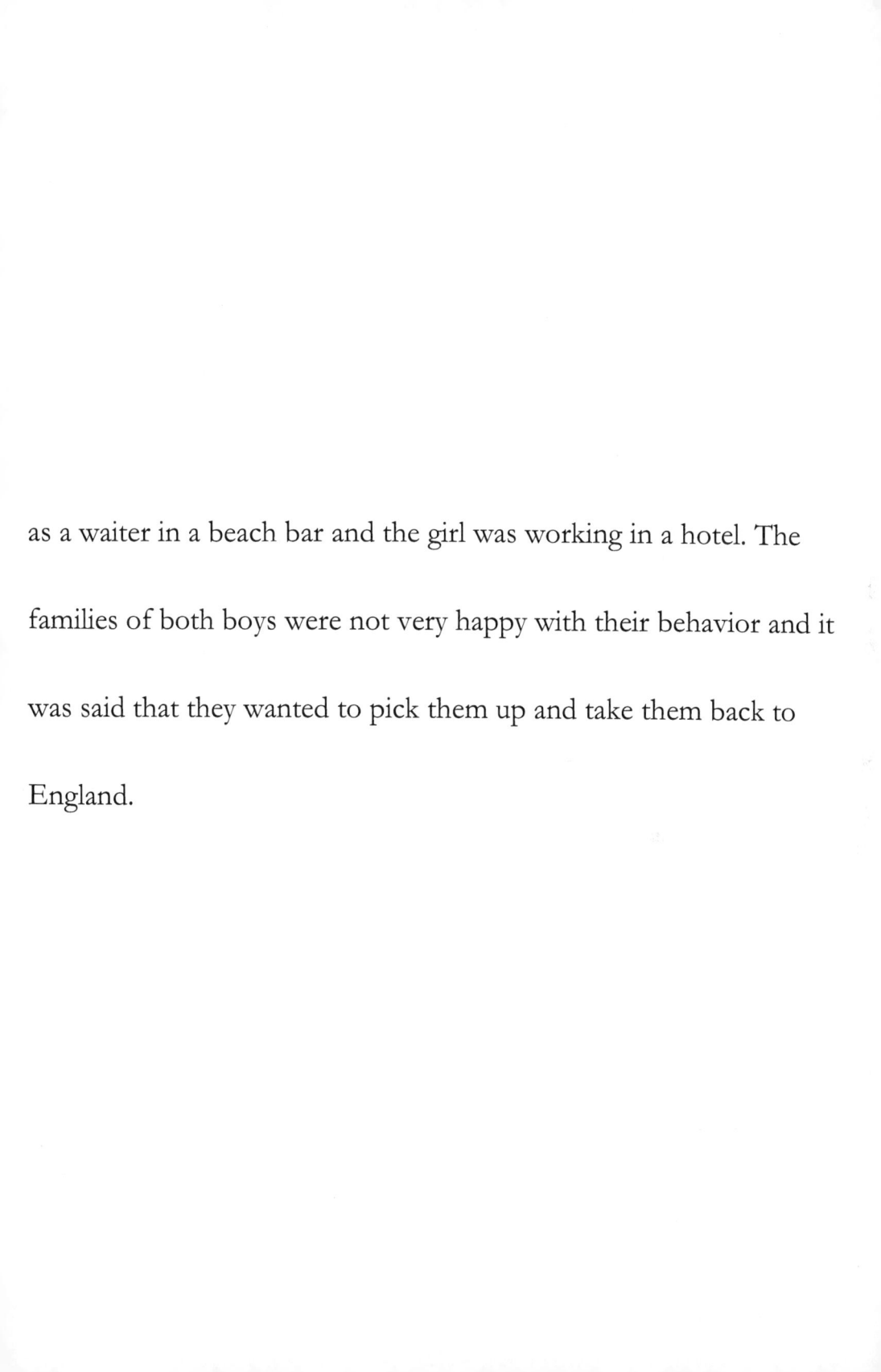

Chapter 14

Felicity was remembering all of this when her brother Tom walked into her room and sat down next to her and asked, "Why don't you come watch one of my games?" and smiling he said, "So I can introduce you to the new coach, tomorrow we have the semi finals and we play at home, come on!!! What do you say?" Felicity looked at him and shrugged, "It's three days before we leave, so why not?

The memories she had just experienced had taken away all the joy she had felt in those days The memory of Andrew had taken away all the happiness she had felt coming home. Tired and sad, she went to bed and told her mother that she was not hungry. She threw herself on the bed and began to cry, she wanted to scream, she wanted revenge now more than ever. She wanted a life worth living, not a life chosen by others, a life that made her feel joy.

The decision to be there in London seemed to her over time to be a decision dictated to her just to be with Andrew, she felt it had not been her complete decision. Felicity promised herself that from now on, every decision would be hers alone, no one and nothing would condition her, life was hers and hers alone.

But was a future in the cafeteria a real thing? Was she ready to take on that responsibility, and London and Sam?

So many unanswered questions, tired she fell asleep while a full moon in the sky watched her from the window, smiling at her and trying to illuminate her face with its rays.

The next morning she showed up at the cafeteria as usual, walked in and saw Norma struggling with the dough for her famous chocolate cakes, there was her apron with her name on it waiting for her, took off her coat, gloves and woollen hat and happily walked towards Norma.

" Good morning Felicity, are you okay? Did you sleep?" Felicity replied smiling, "Of course, tired as I was, I would have slept on the floor too," the two women laughed, "And I know it's tiring work, but you know it gives you so much satisfaction.

Felicity began to help at Norma's direction, but that morning she noticed something strange. Norma, with a mysterious smile on her lips, placed some secret ingredients in the bowl and began to stir vigorously as she worked the dough, a luminous aura seemed to envelop the bowl and the cakes she was preparing.

Felicity, intrigued, watched Norma's gestures carefully. As soon as Norma finished mixing, she added the finishing touch to the cake: a sprinkle of fairy dust. The cake began to glow with a magical light and its fragrance spread throughout the room.

"Norma, what did you just do?" asked Felicity, her eyes filled with wonder.

Norma replied with a sweet smile, "Dear Felicity, my dessert recipes are not like anyone else's. I have special ingredients and ancient magical formulas that allow me to create desserts that bring happiness, magic and wonder to those who eat them."

Felicity was stunned. She could not believe her ears. Every day, with every bite of one of Norma's sweets, she had felt a unique sense of joy and well-being. Now she finally understood why the candy was so magical.

Determined to learn more about these incredible cakes, Felicity asked Norma if she could tell him where this magic came from.

Norma, after baking the two chocolate cakes, took two chocolate cups and some cinnamon cookies, placed them on the large wooden table and said, "Now Felicity, it's time for me to tell you the whole truth about the cafeteria" Felicity, full of curiosity, sat down and looked with her big eyes at the lady in front of her.

"I remember it was Christmas Eve, Carol had bought a nice sweater for her husband and I had bought a book, we were walking when on the steps of the church there was an old lady begging, we approached and Carol saw that she was wearing only a light shawl, and noticing that the poor woman was shivering without a second thought, Carol opened her bag and gave the old lady the sweater she had just bought.

When she saw all this, she was surprised that she had spent almost all her savings to buy it and now she was giving it to a stranger?

But this is the soul of Christmas, later included. The lady took the sweater and looked at her face and smiled.

Suddenly, the lady opened a large bag beside her and took out a book and a red velvet box. She caressed it lovingly and then, looking at us with tear-filled eyes, she handed us the box and said.

"I have waited a long time to find witnesses to this legacy that I received from my grandmother. I could see that you both have big hearts and I am sure that you are the right people to carry on this gift of mine.

Norma paused in her storytelling, you could see she was still excited in the memory, and took a sip of chocolate.

You are two people full of love and opened the box, inside there were glass containers with powders, at that time we had the idea of buying the Cafeteria. After giving us the box, he gave us a book, and when we opened it, we understood that it was a cookbook of sweets," and turning around, he pointed to the book that I had seen on the desk the first day and that was now next to them.

Then she continued, "She explained to us that by putting these ingredients in the dough, the people who would eat the cakes would be happy and peaceful. All the love that Carol had given her by giving her the sweater, she was now giving back to us, but for the whole world. By following the magic cookbook, we know just the right amounts of the magic ingredients.

I will also tell you another secret: the spices never run out, the level of the containers always stays the same".

On the way home that night, we realized that this was a sign that confirmed that the decision to open the cafeteria was the right one.

With you, we can continue to do this and bring a pinch of serenity and happiness with our sweets. You are young and we could spread the magic of our magical sweets all over the world and make the world happier!

Felicity was speechless as she listened to the story, now it was even harder to make a choice so she began to cry, Norma came over and held her close "Felicity what is it tell me?" she looked up and wiped away her tears she said in a low voice "I don't know what to do, I am very undecided, I don't know if I should go back to London or stay.here." Norma stroked her and told him, "You will see that you will understand, life gives us signals and we have to catch them and understand them by listening to them with the HEART".

Felicity was impressed and looked at her in wonder, "Listen with your heart," she repeated in a low voice.

They drank their cocoa in silence, then Norma went into the hall and began to turn on the lights and bring out the blackboard with the day's menu written on it. Felicity started to turn on the coffee machine and put all the croissants and cakes that had just been taken out of the mold on the counter.

The day passed quickly, Mary went to see her and made him a very good espresso, and she was proud of it, she was a fast learner.

"Go on Felicity now comes Jessica will see you tomorrow? " Norma asked.

Felicity nodded with a smile, put on her coat and decided to take her apron home to wash, she put it in her bag and waved goodbye to everyone and walked out.

She started to walk home when she realized she was being followed, she turned around and saw Andrew standing behind her. She stopped and looked at him with a defiant face and asked, "Are you by any chance following me?" The boy looked down at the ground, intimidated by Felicity's unfriendly tone and face, and replied, "Yes, I need to talk to you.

Felicity turned and started walking again and heard "Please I want to explain to you how things went," at that point Felicity stopped, she was curious and so she motioned for Alex to come closer, he approached her with slow and scared steps and started talking.

"Felicity, I'm sorry for what I did, I really wanted to come to you, I swear, in your absence.

I started dating Susan for fun and then it became serious. It was love at first sight, she had become as indispensable to me as air. I couldn't get away from her, she had become like a magnet for me. So I decided to leave with her, I should have called you, I know, but I didn't have the courage. We went to the Bahamas, as you know, as far away from everyone and you as possible, I worked in a beach bar, but I thought of you.

I swear, so many times I would pick up the phone to call you, but then the fear and guilt would take over and I would always put it off until the next day when I would see you in the cafeteria.

One day when I came back from the Bahamas and saw you coming out of the gallery, I stood outside, just like that! I was waiting for you to come out and I saw you in the company of your staff and you looked happy, joking, laughing, and that partly reassured me, I knew you were "over it".

Felicity listened to him, there were a thousand emotions running through her heart, hatred, resentment, sorrow and forgiveness, all these emotions were running together and she did not know which one to choose.

With a knot in her throat, Felicity said, "I suffered a lot, I felt betrayed and mocked, it wasn't easy for me to move on, but I couldn't do anything else, luckily I found someone to take your place in the apartment, because' with the rent I wouldn't have made it. I had to stay in London, although sometimes I would go back home. I couldn't leave everything I had responsibilities and then I thought that coming home would make me think of you and us again.

Because of you I stayed away from men, I didn't want to suffer anymore I was always alone. Just work friends and that's all. This fear of suffering I still carry inside me, I became very distrustful of men and love and all because of you."

Andrew's face turned red and he put his hands in his pockets and moved the snow with his feet and with his face down he listened to the girl's words, he also felt bad. Seeing her again he had felt in his heart the feeling he had for her and now?

"Well we talked now I have to go I have a lot of things to do. Ah Andrew! Next time you want to know something about me, ask me personally and don't bother Mary, okay? Try to be a man!" At these words Andrew looked up and stormed off in a huff. As she watched him run away, she wondered how she could have fallen in love with a boy like him. Shaking her head she started walking home, finally the past was truly behind her, looking at him and talking to him she understood that she felt nothing for him anymore.

She realized that he was an immature boy and that she had been a fool to trust him. Now all those feelings of guilt and fear had to dissolve inside her. She was not to blame for what had happened, she was just a victim of an illusion of love. Andrew would never grow up, he would always be a child.

Understanding this made her feel stronger and more open to new love.

 Soft snow fell from the sky, he looked up and smiled serenely at his new future.

CHAPTER 15

Felicity joined the many spectators who crowded the rink on this cold, frosty evening. The sound of skis whizzing across the ice joined the clatter of hockey sticks on the surface.

Wearing warm hats, scarves, and gloves, the fans clustered around the rink, vying for the best seats near the railing so they could best admire the players' wondrous moves. Felicity stood on the side of the field, watching as Tom warmed up with his teammates, ready for the battle ahead.

Just during the warm-up practice, Felicity admired Alex, the coach, instructing the players in an authoritative voice; his smile and firm, authoritative temperament attracted the attention of Felicity, who in her heart of hearts hoped to have a chance to have a few words with him after the game.

The game began with another thunderous blast of the referee's whistle. The players sprinted off, the puck moving frantically from one side of the rink to the other, sticks clattering against the icy surface, snowflakes flying in the air. Felicity watched with admiration and trepidation as her brother struggled to keep up with his opponents.

As the game progressed , Alex proved to be a skilled and decisive coach. Whenever a player on his team made a mistake, he was there ready to intervene with precise instructions and strong motivation. Alex's words and instructions gave the players with a much needed boost to improve their performance.

Tom and his teammates battled hard to maintain control of the puck and score the coveted point. The game became more and more exciting and the crowd erupted in a chorus of cheers.

At one point, Tom, who was fighting passionately on the field, magically managed to parade toward the opposing goal. With a powerful stick shot, he sent the flying puck past the goalie and into the net. An unstoppable roar of joy erupted from the crowd, and Felicity cheered with all her might, proud of her brother.

After the game, Felicity waited outside the field for her brother; he arrived happily, with Alex by his side, and the girl's heart began to beat faster. Suddenly she was afraid and thought of running away, but her brother, seeing her, called her, "Felicity, come, let me introduce you to our coach," at these words she tried to smile, although inside she regretted having stayed there, she was afraid. They reached Felicity and Alex gave him her hand and said smiling, "But you're the girl from the cafeteria, aren't you?" she blushed smugly that he remembered her and replied, "Yes, I'm Felicity, Tom's sister.

replied sheepishly: "Of course I know. You have a brother who is really a champion, and you expect great things from him. At that moment, they looked into each other's eyes, and there was a spark of attraction between them. Feeling this strength, they both lowered their eyes in embarrassment as Tom looked at them with a smug smile.

"What do you say we go get some pizza?" Tom's voice made the awkwardness that had built up between the two young people disappear, and Alex looked at Felicity and said, "That's fine with me," Felicity, still with the shiver on her skin, replied with a hint of a voice, "Yes, that's fine." All three of them walked to the Italian pizzeria that was located a few blocks away.

Upon entering the diner, they found a small table for three, Felicity stood in front of Alex while Tom stood between them, they ordered three pizzas and beer.

While they waited, Alex began to speak, "Felicity, tell me a little bit about yourself, I know from your brother that you work in an art gallery."

Felicity looked at her brother with a surprised look and replied, "I didn't know I was a subject of yours," Tom tried to explain, "No, and that today while we were changing I mentioned that I had a big sister who was famous in London for her work in one of the most important galleries in London," and then with a stealthy way he made an excuse, getting up and joining some friends at a table near them..

Alex waited for her answer, and as he took a sip of beer, he looked at her with a deep gaze.

"Yes, I work in an art gallery," she said as he stared at her while grabbing a snack, and then Alex replied, "I'm from London, too, but although it's a big and beautiful city, I came here to find some peace and quiet. I needed to get back in the game and decided to train after I hurt my leg.

I didn't want to leave field hockey, and since I couldn't play anymore, it seemed like the obvious alternative, and I have to tell you, Felicity, gives me a lot of satisfaction that I didn't think I had."

Felicity listened to him and realized that he was a very open guy, telling a stranger all this means having a lot of trust in others.

"Alex, you know I have learned that life is full of surprises, and as for London, it was not easy for me to settle in coming from a quiet town like this, but I understand you, I too. Coming back here these days, I appreciate the tranquility of living here, I never would have imagined it, I always dreamed from a young age to take my things and live in London forever, but now that I'm back, I don't feel like going back." Hearing these words, Felicity was surprised at herself.

The pizzas arrived, Tom joined them but took the pizza and moved apologetically to his friends table, Alex and Felicity smiled at each other and began to eat.

They talked about many things, about London and some clubs they both knew and then Alex asked her "Are you engaged?" she got red in the face she felt her cheeks boiling and replied "No not now, I'm very busy with my work I don't have time" he shook his head and replied "For love there is always time. If you can't find it, it's because you want to be alone." When Felicity heard these words, she realized that he was a good guy and very sensitive, so she decided to tell him the truth and replied, "Yes, you're right, I had a bad experience and now I don't feel like committing.

Felicity asked him the same question, "And you Alex, are you engaged?" he gave her a serious look and replied, "You know, I don't know.

It might sound strange, but it is! I left my girlfriend in London, she was against me coming here. When I got hurt, she was worried about getting me a job as a match reporter," he stopped talking and gave a wry smile, then continued, "She is a girl who likes to organize other people's lives. But I had absolutely no desire to sit back and watch other people play, so I asked around and found this opportunity, and overnight I had a job.

I told her that I would be coaching a small team away from London. She got very angry, took all her stuff out of my apartment and left. I haven't seen or heard from her since, so I guess we're on standby for now."

Felicity was surprised that a woman would let a guy like him get away; if it had been her instead of his girlfriend, she would have followed him to the North Pole. But fortunately, not all women are alike.

They finished dinner and walked out of the diner, it was cold, it had stopped snowing, Tom had said goodbye to them and stayed to celebrate the victory with his friends in the diner, so Felicity and Alex walked side by side.

The streetlights lit up the street and the snow sparkled like glitter. As they walked, Felicity shivered. Alex, seeing her shivering, gave her his scarf to cover herself and wrapped it around her neck.

Their faces were very close; the attraction they had felt before returned like lightning, so strong that their mouths touched in a passionate and burning kiss. At that moment, Felicity felt an "emotion she had never felt in her body, invading her with heat, shivers, and an excitement she never thought she would feel. They remained kissing for a few moments. Their mouths were hungry for kisses and they did not want to pull away.

Then Alex took her hand and they looked intensely into each other's eyes and Alex whispered in his ear, "Will you come to my house?" and she answered yes, still aroused from those intense and passionate kisses.

Alex and Felicity walked to his house holding hands, feeling their Intense emotions were spreading among them, a mixture of excitement, happiness and a hint of amazement. Their sweaty palms reflected the strong emotion running through them as their hearts beat in unison, creating a melody of love that echoed in their hearts.

Each time their eyes met as they walked, a spark of passion lit up their eyes as if the stars themselves were present at that moment. In this union, they felt complete, protected and deeply connected to each other, their fingers gently intertwined.

The emotion felt in that handshake was indescribable, a mixture of overwhelming joy and total, unconditional acceptance of the other. At that moment, they both realized that nothing in the world could break that bond. Their hearts beat in unison, and together they felt invincible, ready to face anything next to each other.

The apartment was not far away, and when they arrived, they both felt as if they had flown there.

The apartment was modern, with a white kitchen and a living room with a burning fireplace. They entered, took off their coats, and then Alex made Felicity sit on the white sofa in front of the fireplace. Alex went into the kitchen and returned with a glass of red wine, which they sipped while sitting on the sofa, which Felicity found very comfortable. They remained silent, holding hands.

Felicity loved the intense and passionate way Alex looked at her. They shared funny stories, smiles, and looks full of complicity.

Then Alex turned on the stereo and soft music began to fill the room, creating an even more romantic atmosphere. Felicity and Alex got up from the couch and began to dance slowly, wrapped in each other's embrace.

Their bodies moved together, synchronized, as if this moment was meant to be shared only between them. Alex's hands ran gently down Felicity's back. With this touch, she felt a sense of protection and love. The physical contact increased the intensity between them and the caresses became deeper and more passionate.

Felicity felt her heart beat faster and faster as their intense gazes turned to unstoppable desire. Alex, caught up in the excitement, took her hand and led her to his bedroom.

In the large room was a huge bed with a white leather headboard, at the end of the bed was a mat that was also white, they lay down on the large fur mat and without saying a word, the universe seemed to slow down. Their bodies moved closer to each other as they exchanged tender, passionate kisses.

Every touch, every brush, told of a desire to explore and know the other more deeply. Every little gesture or contact made their bodies vibrate with excitement and made them long to stay in that moment forever, wrapped in that passion so immature but powerful.

They finished making love. They were both out of breath and looked at each other contentedly. They smiled at each other and Felicity said, "Of course field hockey is a great sport. It works your whole body. You are a wonder, Alex." He smiled sheepishly and replied, "Of course you had an insatiable appetite too." She licked her mouth with her tongue, nodded, and looked at him and said, "Shall we do an encore?"

CHAPTER 16

"Hi Felicity, what time are you coming?" the voice or maybe Sam's scream could be heard coming from the phone, at that moment Felicity was serving an espresso with a donut, smiling she thought if she saw what her boss was doing she would faint, but without letting on she replied, "I don't know, you know things are getting long here, tomorrow is the opening of grandma's will and I don't know what to expect" on the other end of the phone there was silence for a few seconds, then a slightly changed voice answered "Don't get smart with me Felicity you are in charge of Willy's Christmas display don't play games because' you know I don't forgive" Hearing these words Felicity rolled her eyes and thought 'what a bitch you are' but not being able to say it she replied 'don't worry about the display I'll be there'.

Then she put down the phone and continued to serve her cappuccinos.

Alex showed up that morning and the looks between them were of passionate fire. She worked the counter and tables, but she felt his gaze on her, as well as his hands the night before; she was excited just to have him around.... Before leaving, Alex told him, "I won't stop thinking about you and your body. I will be waiting for you at my house when you are done." She looked at him with a loving gaze and replied, "I don't stop thinking about you either, I want to be with you. Wait for me," she smiled and walked out of the cafeteria.

Throughout the morning she felt as if she was suspended, lifted off the ground every moment she thought back to the night before, inside she thought she never imagined there could be a man who could give her such intense pleasure and make her feel so good, so complete, so womanly, now she felt more confident about the male gender and about love.

Norma watched her and understood from her demeanor and the way she moved and talked to her clients that she was particularly happy that morning. She felt that Felicity was in a state of grace, perhaps the advice she had given him the day before, about listening to the heart, had been heeded? She was happy about that, she did not know and could not guess what had happened and with whom, but the important thing for Norma was that he felt positive vibes in Felicity for the first time.

On her way home she told her parents that she was going out to dinner with some friends then went to her room to change, shortly thereafter she heard a knock at the door and saw her brother come in and sit down in his chair and in a rather nonchalant way asked

Felicity: "Listen, but what did you and Alex do last night?" the question surprised Felicity and with an angelic look she replied "Nothing, why?" he looked at her with a smile and said "I'm asking because today during practice Alex seemed rather strange, think that instead of calling one of my teammates Paul called him Felicity." She looked at him with an embarrassed look and blushed, then they both laughed, "I guess he has a crush on you..."

Felicity still red in the face and replied, "I don't know, Tom! All I know is that I love it like crazy." He was happy to hear those words. Felicity got up from the chair, kissed him on the cheek, and said, "Good luck, big sister. You deserve it!" and left the room.

Shortly after Alex arrived, "Sorry Ann is a friend of mine can you wait for me in the hall?" she left the doorway with an unnerved look

"And yes, after Andrew, that would be the right revenge for me," she thought as she put on a new black lace leotard and looked smugly at herself in the mirror.

She knocked on the door, but no one answered, so she rang the doorbell. After a while the door opened, but a girl with long red hair appeared. She looked at her curiously and said, "Yes, who are you looking for?" Felicity checked the apartment number, thinking she Alex walked in and said, "She's a friend of mine, come on in," he stared at Felicity, the girl was annoyed, before he went in he said, looking defiantly at Felicity, "Okay, but hurry, I'm hungry," he pushed her away and walked out of the apartment, closing the door behind him. Felicity was speechless the whole time, she stood there looking at him but didn't understand what was going on, "Excuse me, my girlfriend is here now," he said with an annoyed look,

"Perfect timing, I'll call you tomorrow, okay? had made a mistake, but the number was correct. And who was it?

These words struck her in the center of her heart. Like her girlfriend?

See you tomorrow? So was the girl going to stay with him?

Feeling like a second choice, she ran toward the stairs without saying a word and went down without looking back.

A feeling of fear assailed Felicity, a fear that the presence of Alex's girlfriend would jeopardize their relationship. There was also concern that Alex might still have feelings for her. Many questions crowded the girl's mind as she ran and ran from everything and everyone.

CHAPTER 17

"Alex, my love, I missed you so much." Ann's voice echoed in the living room, Alex had not expected it, it had been a surprise for him too, that afternoon he had prepared a little dinner for himself and Felicity, he had been thinking about her all day. While he had been cooking, he had heard the doorbell and had opened it happily, thinking that he would see Felicity. Instead, there was Ann with a suitcase looking at him with a big innocent smile on her face and now?

All this he thought as he looked indifferently at the girl who had once made his heart beat, and in his mind he pondered how he could have fallen in love with such a woman.

How could he have allowed himself to be dominated and conditioned by such a person who he now considered useless, arrogant, and superficial?

"You don't tell me anything, you just stand there and look at me with that empty look like you see a ghost," she said, sitting with her legs crossed in a rather sexy way. She was wearing a black leather suit and very high heels, if he had seen her dressed like that once, Alex would have felt aroused and would have taken her to bed right away, but now he felt nothing, rather he was irritated by this way of being and this so arrogant and haughty way of talking as if she was the smartest one of all.

She used to be able to put up with it and overlook it but now she saw things differently, maybe being away and meeting Felicity had opened her mind and new horizons and she thought "Who does she think she is, just because' she is the daughter of one of the most important politicians in London she thinks she can boss everyone around."

"Yes, Ann, I am looking at a ghost, for me you are now ... you disappeared without saying a word to me. You didn't return my calls and messages. And after a few months you show up here as if nothing happened?" As he said these words inside, he felt lightened, "Ann, don't act like that, there's nothing between us anymore, at least on my part. In this time I've been alone, I've realized that my life is at a turning point, I'm finally doing something I love and that makes me feel fulfilled, and it won't be you or anyone else who takes me back to my old life. In this small town I feel at home, everyone greets me, I am somebody and not a number like in the big cities, here I feel important and loved. and happy with this feeling, he continued to speak with more vigor.

"Then, heading for the front door, he concluded, "And one more thing, I met a woman here for the first time who really makes my heart beat, and I am convinced that it is true love. Having said that,

I would be grateful if you would take your things and your nice leather suit and leave." And very calmly he took Ann's suitcase, which was still intact, opened the front door and put it outside, then turned to the woman who was looking at him in disbelief and motioned for her to leave.

And very calmly he took Ann's suitcase, which was still intact, and opened the front door and put it outside, then he turned to the woman who was looking at him in disbelief and waved her out.

"You'll regret this, don't ever go back to London, you won't find work, my father will take care of it and ruin your career, you're a failure," he said and walked out.

Alex said before closing the door, "I was a failure to be with you," and slammed the door in his face.

CHAPTER 18

Felicity ran out of the building where Alex lived, her heart pounding, she was out of breath. Not knowing where to go, she began to run, a few tears wetting her face, and inside she felt so much sadness. How could she trust him? How could she think he was different? But in her heart, she could not hate him. She had felt things with him that she could only imagine. But what could she do now? Go back to her job in London?

No, no, it could not end like this. Suddenly she stopped and she found herself at a fork in the road, one road leading to her home and the other leading to the cafeteria. She stopped and closed her eyes, took a long breath and tried to feel the beating of her heart, which was now very fast, and thought, "Listen to your heart," as Norma had told her. Listen to it, push everything out of your mind, thoughts, fears, stay in silence and listen to that little voice that we all have and that tells us when to follow her. He remained with his eyes closed for a few seconds, then opened them again and took the road leading to the cafeteria. From a distance he saw that it was closed, looked at his watch, and thought that Norma must have closed earlier that evening. She walked over and took from the hiding place the key to open the cafeteria, and with trembling hands went inside. She walked to the kitchen and turned on the lights.

The room that presented itself to her was spotless, everything was in order, even the pots and utensils had been cleaned and put in their place, on the work table Felicity strangely found the cookbook, Norma had not put it back in its secret place at the end of the evening. Felicity wondered why it was there that night? It was as if the book was calling to her with uncertain steps as she approached the cookbook.

Her hands began to tremble. She was excited. Suddenly a gust of wind came from the door and Felicity opened the cookbook, her eyes filled with wonder as she read the recipe, and at that moment her heart stopped.

The recipe was called "True Love Cake" and she began to quickly read the process and the ingredients, at the end, as she had seen with Norma, there was the magic touch, the magic powder that was sprinkled on the dough before it was baked.

Quickly agility, she put on apron and began to arrange all the necessary ingredients on the worktable, starting with the flour, then the sugar, which she mixed carefully with her hands, then the eggs and a drop of milk, a bit of butter melted beforehand and started to knead, then the yeast.

Where could the magic powder be? Felicity looked around desperately, if she could not find the magic powder, everything would be useless. She had to make this cake to find out what to do, to find out what her future would be.

She started to open the doors and looked under the kitchen utensils, in the pantry and then she opened Norma's closet and there she saw a picture of her and her grandmother which she admired fondly and she took it and there she noticed that right behind the picture was a medium sized box, it was red velvet, she remembered the story that Norma told and thought that the box must have been this one, but it had a padlock with a combination to open it. Felicity saw the padlock and looked up. What is it now?

She could not find the combination; it was impossible. She looked at her dough on the table; it was ready, and she had even found the heart shape as it was written in the cookbook. She had to give up?

"I can't do this," Felicity said as she held the box in her hands.

Suddenly she had the impression that her grandmother was there with her, she could smell her scent and feel her presence grandmother help me ..Please help me....

He sat down on the floor of the large kitchen and began to cry. It was all over !With this cake she would understand whether Alex loved her or not. By now she was certain, so many were the doubts that came to her.

Dejected, she put the box in the closet when she suddenly remembered the numbers her grandmother liked to play in the Christmas lottery.

A light illuminated her memory and so she placed the red box on the table and began to enter the numbers in an ascending order 1 - 12-25 and suddenly the lock opened....

Inside, she found little bottles of many colors with unintelligible names. Felicity reread the recipe, took the appropriate bottle, took a pinch, and spread it over the top of the cake.

The stove was hot, Norma kept it lit all the time, turned up the fire and, after waiting for it to reach the desired temperature, baked the heart. Suddenly, the tall flames embraced the cake and seemed to dance with the heart. She looked in amazement at what was happening, then went back to finish reading the cookbook, and there it was written in big letters that those who wanted to know if they were loved by a REAL love should eat the hot cake and not let it cool, Felicity thought, "hot as love."

When the cake was ready, she put it on the counter, cut off a slice, and ate it while it was still warm, risking a burn. After eating it, she suddenly felt happy and euphoric, as if she were drunk.

Felicity thought she had done something wrong and, staggering, she sat down in the chair and closed her eyes. There she had a vision.

As if in a dream, Felicity saw herself on a long avenue, there was someone beside her, but she could not quite see who it was...then suddenly, at the end of the avenue, she saw her grandmother smiling at her and motioning for him to come to her. Felicity quickened her Grandma told her, "Listen to your heart." After saying this she took her hands and motioned for her to look next to her, Felicity turned and saw Alex smiling and looking at her lovingly, then Felicity looked at her grandmother again and nodded her head.pace and caught up to her and hugged her.

Then Grandmother said, "Magic is the love you feel when you find your soul mate... ...." Suddenly, she opened her eyes again and was surprised to see Alex standing in front of her, looking at her just like in her dream.

Surprised, she stood up and hugged him tightly, then pulled herself away with difficulty. Alex kissed her with all the passion that could exist between two people in love.

"Don't ever leave me again, do you understand? Now that I have found you, I don't want to lose you to anyone or anything. You have given me so much love in one day that no one has ever been able to give me in my whole life.

After they kissed, Alex took her face in his hands and whispered,

Felicity smiled with tears in her eyes and said "I was afraid I had lost you, I thought you were back with your girlfriend" Alex hugged her and said "No love, I feel in my heart that you are the most beautiful gift life has ever given me and will always be!!!" Felicity started to cry she could not stop it was a dream after suffering so much for love to hear those words now with Alex she would have her REVIVAL.

They remained embraced in silence, their hearts beating in unison, then Felicity broke away from this embrace so warm and passionate and said, "My Christmas present is you and you will be forever".

The light in her eyes was of passion and love, that love you meet once in a lifetime and understand immediately because you feel it is special, unique and forever...

Felicity looked at the cookbook and smiled, and in her heart she made the most important decision of her life.

In that moment in Alex's arms, everything became clear in her mind: she would continue to work in the cafeteria and stay in her town.

Grandma's house had been left to her, so she decided to renovate it and move in with Alex as man and wife.

Sam knew that her choice would have called her out and showered her with insults, but she no longer cared about the gallery and London.

Her future was in her small town, and with Norma's help and entrepreneurial skills, she would share the recipes for Norma's Cafeteria's magical cakes with the world, spreading some joy and love around the world.

From that day forward, Felicity and Norma continued to work together to make the magical pies. Like Norma, Felicity learned the secret ingredients and magic formulas that made these cakes unique in the world.

With her newfound knowledge, Felicity became a great pastry chef and helped spread the magic of Norma's magical sweets around the world.

Felicity made the world a sweeter place, full of joy and magic. And it all started in Norma's little kitchen, where a girl in love listened to her heart and followed her dreams and the magic of love.

Follow me on my blog: selvaggiastark.blogspot.com

I would love to hear what you think.

Printed in Great Britain
by Amazon